# THE WITCH'S FACE

## A Mexican Tale

adapted by Eric A. Kimmel

illustrated by Fabricio Vanden Broeck

Holiday House/New York

Para David Martinez y todos mis amigos en Guadalajara.

E.A.K.

Para la Pitzi y los Goritos.

F.V.B.

Text copyright © 1993 by Eric A. Kimmel
Illustrations copyright © 1993 by Fabricio Vanden Broeck
Printed in the United States of America
First Edition

Library of Congress Cataloging-in-Publication Data
Kimmel, Eric A.
The witch's face : a Mexican tale / by Eric A. Kimmel ;
illustrated by Fabricio Vanden Broeck.—1st ed.
p.  cm.
Summary: Don Aurelio falls in love with a witch who has a
beautiful face but fails to heed her special instructions.
ISBN 0-8234-1038-2
[1. Folklore—Mexico.]  I. Broeck, Fabricio Vanden, 1954–, ill.
II. Title.
PZ8.1.K56Wi    1993
398.22—dc20    92-44380    CIP    AC    [E]

This retelling of "The Witch's Face" is partly based on "La Esposa Bruja," a story from the oral tradition of the Mazahua Indians of Central Mexico. A Spanish version of the story appears in Lilian Scheffler's collection, *Cuentos y Leyendas de México: Tradición Oral de Grupos Indígenas y Mestizos*, published in 1982 by Panorama Editorial of Mexico City. Other elements of the story are the fruit of a delightful evening in Guadalajara. I owe thanks to my friend and colleague, Dr. David Martinez, his cousins, and his students at the University of Guadalajara for sharing their knowledge of Mexican witch tales and traditions.

*Eric A. Kimmel*

**M**any years ago a young gentleman named Don Aurelio Martinez set out on horseback for Mexico City. As it grew dark, he began looking for a place to spend the night. He saw a light in the distance. "Perhaps I can find a bed there," Don Aurelio thought as he spurred his horse forward.

In a while he came to a large house built of black stones. A lantern hung above the doorway. Don Aurelio dismounted and tied his horse to a tree.

He knocked on the door.

"*¡Buenas noches!*" he called out cheerfully. "Is anyone home?"

The door opened.

Three women stood in the doorway. One was dressed entirely in black, with a lace shawl pulled over her head. The second, blond and plump, wore a canary yellow skirt and jangly brass bracelets. The third, the youngest and most attractive, was dressed in a simple cotton frock embroidered with birds and flowers. Her hair hung down her back in two braids. It struck Don Aurelio that the three women had the same face: old, young, and middle-aged. It was as if he were meeting the same person at three different times of her life.

"Come in," the women said, as if they had been expecting him.

They led him to a room where he found a table set with a platter of enchiladas and a cup of pulque. As Don Aurelio sat down, the youngest whispered in his ear, "Beware. All is not as it seems."

"Pardon?" Don Aurelio replied. But the girl acted as if she had said nothing. *This is all very strange*, Don Aurelio thought, as he waited for the others to sit down.

"Won't you join me?" he asked.

"We have already eaten," they
answered.

The youngest stared at Don Aurelio.
Her mysterious beauty fascinated him.
He could not take his eyes from her face.

He finished the enchiladas and drank the pulque.
Within minutes a great weariness engulfed him.
Don Aurelio leaned back in his chair. His eyes closed.
He knew nothing more.

He awoke to find the sun going down. He had slept through the night and the entire next day. The three women were setting the table.

"Why did you not wake me?" he asked them.

"You were weary. It is good that you slept. Now it is time for dinner," they answered.

"Surely you will join me," Don Aurelio replied.

"We already ate," the oldest one told him. But when she looked away, the youngest whispered in his ear, "Drink nothing. Your life depends on it."

"Why?" he murmured in a low voice so the others could not hear.

But she said nothing more.

This time Don Aurelio ate the enchiladas, but he only pretended to drink the pulque. A few minutes later he fell back in his chair with his eyes closed.

"Does he sleep?" the old one asked.

"Like the dead," the one with the bracelets replied.

The three went into the kitchen, shutting the door behind them.

Don Aurelio tiptoed to the kitchen door as soon as they were gone. Looking through the keyhole, he saw them uncover four jars. The first contained snakes. The second, lizards. The third, spiders, and the fourth, hideous to describe, cockroaches! The two older women smacked their lips with relish as they swallowed the creatures whole. Then they passed around a jug and drank until their mouths were red. It was not wine that stained their lips, but blood.

"*¡Madre de Díos!*" Don Aurelio gasped. "They are witches!" But he also noticed that while the youngest woman ate and drank with the others, she did so without pleasure.

As soon as the witches finished eating, they opened the cupboard and brought out three pairs of straw wings, which they tied to their shoulders. Then, as Don Aurelio watched in amazement, they pulled off their faces and buried them in a sack of cornmeal.

"The hour is late. We must go," the old one screeched. Her luminous eyes lit the darkness as the witches spread their wings and vanished into the night.

Don Aurelio recoiled from the horror he had seen. He tripped over a chair in the darkness and fell, striking his head against the table. The room turned blacker than a night without stars. Don Aurelio's eyes closed. He knew nothing more.

Don Aurélio awoke at dawn, his head throbbing, to find himself imprisoned in an iron cage. The young witch stood on the other side of the bars. She stared at Don Aurelio, her eyes filled with sorrow. "Why didn't you escape while we were away last night? It is too late now. You are doomed."

Don Aurelio reached out to her through the bars. "Tell me your name."

"I am Emilia."

"Are you a witch too, Emilia?"

She shook her head. "No. Not until tomorrow night, when I take my final vows. You will die, and I must be the one to take your life. There is no other way."

"But there is!" Don Aurelio pleaded. "Emilia, I cannot believe that you want to be a witch. Why else would you attempt to protect me? I saw what happened last night. I saw you hide your face and fly away. Your mother and grandmother may be witches, but you are not like them. There is still compassion in your heart. I can feel it. Do not let it die, Emilia. Let us escape together. Help me, Emilia, so that I can help you."

A glimmer of hope flickered across Emilia's face. She looked around to be sure they were alone. Satisfied, she took a key from her apron and passed it through the bars. "Stay here until we leave tonight. You know where we hide our faces. Take mine. Burn the others. Mother and Grandmother cannot pursue us without their faces. Another pair of wings is hanging in the cupboard. It has enough magic to last one night. The wings will carry you home. My witch's face will protect you from whatever evil you may encounter along the way. However, you must burn it the moment you reach safety. Promise me that."

Don Aurelio swore he would.

"Then, make a new face for me. It need not be beautiful. Any face is better than the face of a witch. When the new face is finished, call my name. The spells that bind me will break and I will come to you." Just then they heard someone coming. "I must go," Emilia said. "Remember. Burn my face." She kissed Don Aurelio through the bars and hurried away.

That night the two older witches mocked Don Aurelio. "You should have fled while you had the chance, Mortal!" they cackled. Emilia said nothing. Her eyes met Don Aurelio's for an instant, then moved away.

As soon as the witches left, Don Aurelio unlocked the door. He pulled the three faces from the sack of cornmeal, put Emilia's in his pocket, and dropped the others into the stove. They flared up like tissue paper. Within seconds they had burned to ashes.

A rush of cold air swept through the room as Don Aurelio slipped on the straw wings. He glided through the kitchen window. Soon he was soaring through the night sky.

Don Aurelio reached his home at midnight. Slipping the wings from his shoulders, he hurried across the courtyard to the stable. He lit a candle. But when he held Emilia's face to the flame, its mysterious beauty so haunted him that he could not bring himself to destroy it.

Instead, he slipped it back into his pocket. Taking knife, awl, and needle, he sewed a scrap of leather into a face. Unfortunately, his skill did not equal his ambition. The face's eyes were crooked, its nose was a shapeless lump, its mouth a slit, and its ears two ragged flaps hurriedly basted on.

But at the time Don Aurelio hardly noticed these flaws. It was dark, and he was in a hurry to bring Emilia to him.

"Emilia," he whispered.

The next moment he held her in his arms. She took the leather mask from his hands and pressed it against her cheeks. "You are all I have now. Do not forsake me," she whispered to Don Aurelio as they embraced. The candlelight fell across Emilia's new face. Don Aurelio shuddered. "Do not pity me," Emilia told him. "It brings me great joy to know I am free of the witches. Does it matter what my face looks like?"

Don Aurelio answered no. But in his heart he was less sure of that reply than he might have been.

The next morning Don Aurelio introduced Emilia to his family. He described how they met in the market in Mexico City where Emilia had a booth selling straw wings and other toys for children. They had fallen in love and wished to be married. His mother and sisters welcomed Emilia, although they could not help staring at her misshapen face.

Don Aurelio's father greeted Emilia politely. "My house is your house," he said. He ordered his servants to prepare the guest room for her and to see to her comfort. But he said nothing about a wedding.

A month passed. Emilia's presence brightened the household. She played with Don Aurelio's younger sisters and helped them with their lessons. She sat with Don Aurelio's mother by the hour, playing the guitar while Señora Martinez worked on her embroidery. She even accompanied the family to church.

Even so, Don Aurelio's father remained distant. His few conversations with Emilia were never more than polite. He sat at the dinner table, observing her as one might observe an odd insect that accidentally flew through the window. If he had any thoughts, he shared them with no one.

Was it his father's reaction or something else that made Don Aurelio grow more unsettled as the weeks passed? He caught himself looking away whenever he and Emilia were together. "This is foolish. I love the person, not the face," he told himself over and over again. But that twisted mask hung in his thoughts like a flock of ravens circling in the sky.

One evening, as Don Aurelio prepared for bed, his father came to his room.

"This joke has gone on long enough," Señor Martinez said sternly. "Who is this woman? How did you meet her? I demand to know."

"I have told you already."

"You have told me nothing! Where is your horse? Don't say you left it in Mexico City. I wrote to your friends there. They say you never arrived."

"I love Emilia," Don Aurelio insisted.

His father sneered. "Love? I could understand if she were a beauty. But when a young man of good family falls in love with a freak, he is either insane or bewitched."

"You are mistaken, Father," Don Aurelio insisted.

"Then tell me the truth!"

"I cannot."

Señor Martinez stormed from the room, leaving Don Aurelio alone with his thoughts.

"It is the face," Don Aurelio decided at last. "Father would have no doubts if Emilia were beautiful. Nor would I," he admitted with a sinking heart. "That is the solution. Emilia had a beautiful face once. I must give it back to her."

Don Aurelio slipped on his coat and hurried along the hallway until he reached the guest room.

He found the door slightly ajar. He peered inside. Moonlight streamed through the open window. Two pairs of straw wings hung on the wall above Emilia's bed. Her hair spread out over the pillow like fine lace. But the face in the moonlight was as worn as a piece of old leather.

Don Aurelio gently removed the leather mask. He took the witch face from his pocket and smoothed it over Emilia's cheeks. "The witches can never find you here. You need hide your beauty no longer." Don Aurelio bent down to kiss her forehead.

Emilia's eyes opened. She glanced in the mirror. "You promised to burn it! Why did you break your promise?" she shrieked in horror when she saw her face. She leaped from the bed before Don Aurelio could answer. "I understand now. You never loved me. It was the face you loved, though you knew it was the face of a witch. Very well, since it is a witch you want, then a witch I will be. But know this: a witch can never love a mortal man." So saying, she snatched up her wings and flew out the window.

"Emilia!" Don Aurelio lunged after her. In desperation, he slipped on the
second pair of wings and tried to follow. But whatever magic they held was
long gone. With a cry, Don Aurelio fell to the courtyard.

Don Aurelio lived for many years, although he never walked again. Nor did he ever marry. Still and all, he had a distinguished career as a judge and senator. That peculiar leather mask, though, never left his side. Sometimes, when he thought himself alone, he was seen holding it in his lap and calling for someone named Emilia. But though he called her name a thousand times, she never came.

Before he died, he asked that these words be carved upon his tombstone:

*La cara bonita es la cara amada,*
*aunque esté hecha de cuero.*

(A beautiful face is one which is loved, even if it is made of leather.)